PHASES OF GAGE

After the Accident Years

by

LISA REDFERN

Lisa Redfern

Library of Congress Control Number: 2017914783

Published in the United States by Little Mountain Publishing

ISBN: 0-9655998-8-4
ISBN-13: 978-0-9655998-8-7

Phases of Gage

DEDICATION

This book is dedicated to those who have experienced a traumatic injury.

Your courage to heal and re-learn how to live
is a testament to the
strength of the human spirit.

It is also dedicated to caregivers who
support folks while in recovery and beyond.

Your patience, love, and encouragement
are generous gifts that increase in valuable
with time and distance.

CONTENTS

ILLUSTRATIONS

Point of View & Spelling Adaptation Notes:

Changes of point of view are indicated by the following images and fonts.

Phoebe **Leander**

Phineas Gadugi

David Arial Narrow

Narration: Times New Roman

Republic of Chile Orthography Note: 'Chili' spelling within the text of Phases of Gage comes from the 1850 Mitchell Map of South America. "…theories say Chile may derive its name from a Native American word meaning either 'ends of the earth' or 'sea gulls'… from the Mapuche word *chilli,* which may mean 'where the land ends….' -- Wikipedia

PHOTO CREDIT: JEDIMENTAT44

Introduction

On the day of Phineas's accident, a thirteen-pound
tamping iron entered beneath his right cheek. It punched
a hole through the frontal lobe of his brain and exited at
the top of his head.

Since 1867, his skull and tamping iron have been on
display at the Warren Anatomical Museum in Boston,
Massachusetts.

Phoebe

The Accident 1848

Fighting to Survive

Phin was hurt—bad—in an explosion on the railroad site.

As soon as word reached us in Lebanon, Uncle Edward rode with Mother through the night to get to Phin.

Cavendish, Vermont, where Phin rents a room, is thirty-six miles from our home in New Hampshire. When Mother arrived, Phin was bleeding, coughing, and sneezing; he was spitting up blood.

Despite Phin's condition, he recognized Mother; even greeting her with an apologetic smile.

Dr. Harlow told Mother that when he fished for bone fragments, he put his fingers all the way through my brother's head.

He admitted surprise when Phineas remained awake, saying that he didn't feel anything.

Mother saw the boys on Phin's gang when they came to check on him. Phin had recruited most of them from home.

A few days after Mother's arrival, Phineas slipped into a delirium. She spent eleven days watching over him. Dr. Harlow said we couldn't bring him home. He was too fragile to move.

By some miracle or our fervent prayers, Phineas came out of the fever. He didn't know how much time had passed.

Joe, one of the gang boys, brought Mother home. She looked haggard; there were dark circles under her eyes. Joe told us, "Dr. Harlow said Mrs. Gage has to rest. She hasn't been eating or sleeping, and she can't stop crying. The Doctor wants to know if another family member can come to help?"

Before he left, Joe gave us the news that Phineas lost the sight in his left eye.

He said that the Doctor wouldn't say what he thought of Phin's chances. Joe gave a sad chuckle when he relayed Phin's pronouncements that he'd be back to work in a few days.

ꊁꊁꊁ

Father decided that I would take Mother's place in Cavendish.

Where others are squeamish with the necessary tasks of nursing, I can do it without fail. On our farm and among our neighbors, I'd seen my share of injuries, illnesses, and death.

I set my brother Dexter's arm when he broke it falling out of the hay loft. His screams were so loud; I was sure the folks in the next county thought I was committing murder.

I stayed with Priscilla Kernan when she had dysentery with a foul smelling, bloody flux. I washed her and her bedclothes so many times that I thought about making her sleep inside the wash tub.

A year after Priscilla's dysentery, I was with her when she went into labor. Her little girl was born blue and deformed. Priscilla had wanted to hold her baby, but I covered it up, hiding its grotesque face, setting it on the sideboard in a hurry. By then, I had seen that Priscilla's womanly parts followed the baby into the outside world.

We buried poor Priscilla with her stillborn baby cradled over her heart.

Father says, "In some ways Daughter, you are more like one of my sons." This is because I don't cry.

᠊᠊᠊

I thought I was ready to see Phin. But I wasn't. My brother looked bruised, beat-up, and grossly misshapen. The bandages covering his head were soiled, in need of change. The room was hot. I gagged when the sick-sweet smell got into my nose. It hit the back of my tongue, causing immediate cramping in my belly.

Seeing him so savagely wounded drained my breath, rattled my bones and turned my muscles into jiggling jelly. I clapped a hand tightly over my mouth, resisting the sudden, forward surge of my neck and head.

I wanted to run to the outhouse, but Phin's good eye was locked onto me.

Father and I listened to the Dr. ask, "Can you name these people?" he pointed to Father and me.

"Father! And Phebes!" Phineas said. "I wish my room were more presentable," he swept his arm out, motioning to the stained linens, "but I have been busy."

"Don't get up!" Father said in a strained voice as he rushed forward, grasping Phineas on the shoulder. Phin didn't seem to notice Father's pained expression. He took Father's hand all the while looking at me. "Come on over Phebes, I got the crap knocked out of me, but I won't bite."

"Phineas Prichard Gage! Injured or not, that is no way to speak in front of your sister!"

"The devil got into me, Old Man," Phineas said, "when that son-of-a-bitch tamkin iron went through my head."

Father grew red in the face. I couldn't help giggling. Phin would never have spoken to him that way before. But the sparkle in his eye told me he was still my brother. Phineas held out a hand. I walked over, taking it.

His grip was warm and firm. He tried to wink the way he used to, but it was such a weak attempt that it made me laugh again. The fear that had risen within me calmed.

When Father was ready to leave, I walked him back to the livery. I'd never seen him cry before. I turned away.

"Daughter, you must do as your mother asked," Father instructed as he prepared to leave.

I nodded, I'd do what I could.

When I returned to Phin's room, he was dozing. Doctor Harlow sent me to wash the soiled linens. Dried blood had stiffened on the bandages. I'd seen that before. But smelling the rancid, jelly-like globs clinging to them hit me like a hard, punch in the gut.

Mr. Adams, the tavern owner, let me use the stove in the kitchen to boil water. When it was hot, I filled a tub out back.

In the crisp night air, with my forearms submerged in what resembled a bucket of blood, I fully realized the extent of my brother's injury.

Every bit of that gore came out of my big brother's head. Surely, he couldn't survive! And if he did... If he did... My tears dropped into the wash tub as I scrubbed.

Before Doctor Harlow left that night, he told me to keep ice water close by in case a fever came up again. Once he was gone, I fed Phineas some soup. He said it was tasteless. When I tried it, I thought it was flavorful. I didn't tell him that but kept encouraging him to eat.

As he was falling asleep, we quietly recalled memories from home. Phineas had a talent with people—he was the one who saw how skilled our brother Dex had become with woodworking. It was Phineas who convinced Father to send Dexter to work in Uncle Herbert's furniture shop. Phineas could always choose the right person for the right job when he organized work crews.

"That's why you're here, Phebes," Phin yawned, "you're tough, you can stomach the rot. You should have seen Mother."

Smiling, I patted his hand, he was right, mother was more delicate than me. Nursing him the last few weeks had to have been difficult for her.

I nodded off in my chair. Somewhere around 11:30 p.m., I woke. Phineas was jerking in his sleep. I spoke to him. He groaned. I asked if he was alright. I had to yell at him before he opened his eye. He slurred, "Leave ee, 'lone."

When I felt his forehead, it was burning hot! My hands trembled as I bathed his face with cool water. The night seemed like it would never end.

When the Doctor arrived the next morning to examine Phin, he poked at his face, frowning, "The swelling has increased. You should have sent for me," he criticized. "Didn't you notice his eye protuberance?

Or the flush on his neck?"

Addled from lack of sleep, I bristled at the Doctor's critical tone. "Candlelight wouldn't show the color of his skin."

Phineas fell into a coma. His blind eye looked like a toad's; his forehead was puffy. His breath stank worse than a dung pile.

נ נ נ

When Phin's railroad gang stopped by to visit, they were sad to see the downturn in his condition. It went without saying that we thought our time there had turned into a death watch.

Shamus, Phin's closest friend, asked me to step outside when it looked like the Grim Reaper started scratching at the door. He took measurements of Phineas so the cabinet maker could start building us a box.

Pulling out Phin's Sunday best, I brought his jacket to my nose. The smell brought up feelings of safety and protection. My oldest brother was my champion. I mourned, not only for myself and the family but for Caroline too.

She was the girl Phineas had loved since her family moved to the farm next door. Phin and Caroline were like two parts of a whole. I remember when she told me about the first time they kissed, and how she cried when he took the job over in Cavendish. After he moved, she was so busy writing letters to him that we hardly saw her.

Caroline had wanted to come to Phin's side after the accident, but Phineas and mother had forbidden it. Phin didn't want her to see him damaged and Mother said that his care was strictly a family matter.

חחח

Two days later, Shamus came to say that the coffin was ready. I told Doctor Harlow that I was going to take Phineas home immediately once he died.

Doctor Harlow wasn't ready to give up. When he removed the bandages, he found something growing in the wound.

It looked like glistening, yellow snot down deep in the wet parts. There was a hard, crusty blackness around the edges.

I could see the Doctor's nostrils flaring. An overpowering stench filled the room. I watched as he steeled himself to inspect it closer. "The infection has invaded the sinus cavity; effluent is seeping from the vitreous chamber. Blast! This damned thing will not get the best of me!" he cursed.

I can't say that I've known many doctors, but the ones I've seen usually hold an even temper. Seeing the Doctor's confidence shaken was something I'll never forget.

"My brother is rotting from the inside out," I stated the obvious.

The Doctor glared at me. "Your brother is young and virile. If I can combat the infection, he could still live."

Doctor Harlow used a pair of curved scissors, cutting and scraping away at the fungus. He sprinkled a caustic powder over the raw flesh. "I'm going to relieve the pressure."

"Please, Doctor Harlow," I pleaded, "leave him be, you'll only make his suffering last longer!"

Mrs. Adams, who was helping with the laundering, took up my argument, "He looks as if he has water on the brain. Letting him go to his maker is the kindest way."

"It is not water that is killing him," Doctor Harlow replied, "but matter!"

When the Doctor brought out a scalpel, I shouted, "No!"

Disregarding me, he bent over his patient.

I watched a drop of dark, red blood form beneath the blade near the corner of Phin's eye. It elongated into a straight line, as Doctor Harlow sliced, with a steady hand, a path along the side of Phin's nose. Like two pieces of cloth, separating after a seam ripper gouges through binding threads, the flesh sprang apart.

From the incision erupted a thick river of pus and blood. It stank of filth and death. It ran over the Doctor's hands, into Phin's mouth, and down his neck. It saturated the pillow

before I supplied the cloth. "Bandages, girl!" the Doctor shouted.

I felt myself gagging but kept my teeth clamped tightly so that the Doctor wouldn't see.

〽〽〽

Mother returned. Over the next six days, Phin's' wound drained. Sopping and wiping up the foul, yellowish liquid, washing and drying linens was constant. We were thankful for Mrs. Adams's help.

Mother grew angry when she heard me mention the coffin. "Phoebe, what if Phineas hears?"

Mother turned to Phin, stroking his cheek, "There, there my darling, you are improving every day. We have God and Doctor Harlow to thank for that. You'll be returning home to us in no time."

Mother was right. Phin did come home. He tried picking up where he left off, but I could tell it wasn't easy. Fits of temper at himself weren't like him. Most distressing was his refusal to see Caroline.

Phineas

Ocean Crossing 1852

Four Years After the Accident

I dropped my bags in the small, dimly lit room I would share with Father. The entrance to it was through shutter-like doors at one end of the long Saloon. The Saloon spanned the entire width of the ship. Tables filled the space where passengers would take their meals and socialize. Mother and Phoebe had an identical room across the way.

Running a hand over a decorative stair rail; I took note of the woodwork; it was superb. "Uncle Herbert would appreciate the craftsmanship," I commented. Father agreed.

We joined other passengers on the deck watching the crew scramble as they prepared for launch. The sails unfurled; the yards braced. Jumping like a fish, the Witch of the Wave started our voyage into Southward seas. A cheer from the passengers rose up.

Once land was out of sight, I remained on deck

while the others retreated. Holding tightly to the rail, keeping my gaze on the horizon, I swallowed past the bile that inched its way up my throat.

"It'll be easier if you give in to it, Sir," said a deep voice beside me. To compensate for my one-sided vision, I swung my head around till I could see him. The motion intensified the already tenuous situation in my gut.

To keep my hair from whipping around my face, I keep my hat pulled low. I wear it that way to protect my soft spot and it hides my dead eye. A beard conceals some of the scars.

I was once an arrogant man, confident in my strength, good looks, and wit. In the years since the accident, I've turned into a wallflower, someone who keeps to the shadows. Mother says that I behave like a 'stinking violet.'

The man introduced himself as James McGill. He held out a hand. Unlike most folks who see me for the first time, McGill didn't avoid looking me in the face. His grip was firm. Rough callouses and weathered, leathery skin told me he was someone who spent long hours outside. "Bread, crackers, and water will help with the stomach. By the look of things, you know how to handle adversity."

"Obliged," I replied, clamping my jaw. I turned back

toward the open sea. I could sense Mr. McGill watching me as if he expected more conversation. I ignored him.

Smacking the rail twice with an open hand, McGill said, "Well then... A pleasant voyage to you, Mr. Gage."

If I had known how important McGill was to become to my future, I ask myself— would I have been kinder at our first meeting? Probably not. I was still feeling inferior.

I thought back to when I was well enough to go home. Folks there, who'd known me my entire life, had to get used me. Heck, I had to do the same.

I didn't have anything in common with my old friends anymore; conversations were strained. I couldn't recover the stamina I once had when working in the fields. My fuse was short; my brothers got the brunt of my anger. Everyone who judged me, even about sea sickness, felt its bite.

Dr. Harlow visited a few times. When he observed my frustration, he offered another alternative; travel to Boston. Exhibit myself at the medical college. Mother thought spending time with Dr. Harlow would be good for me. Needing, more than anything, to get away from everything familiar, I agreed.

Dr. Harlow bought me city clothes, put me up in a comfortable hotel, and gave me a meal allowance. In exchange, I allowed myself to be examined, inspected, poked at, prodded and questioned by countless doctors from every conceivable discipline.

Although Dr. Harlow explained my accident and the injury, most of them did not believe it. They claimed it was a hoax. I had my iron with me—even had it engraved. "Evidence" that those egotistical educated men dismissed.

When I couldn't take another day of that, I accepted an offer from P.T. Barnum. I would join his freak show in New York.

My room accommodations at the Union House Hotel were not as pleasant as in Boston, but Barnum paid eighty dollars a week. Barnum's customers would not be allowed to touch me or come closer than a few feet to see the pulse in my brain when I pulled my hair aside.

Barnum promoted me along with George Anderson; Two Wonders of the World - Man with his Brains Blown Out and The Living Skeleton. We were neighbors at the hotel, and we spent time together before and after our exhibits.

George was not well; he only weighed forty-eight pounds. Eating was a problem. Try as he would, solids would not stay down. In a silver flask, that most use for spirits, George carried milk. He sipped on it to keep his strength up.

One day while we sat on a sunny bench in a secluded corner of Central Park, I said, "It doesn't sit well with me, George."

"What's that?"

"The freak show. Behaving like you don't hear the comments. Smiling when you get so mad that you want to curse and hit someone. The customers treat us worse than slaves. Like we're animals, without thoughts or feelings."

"The longer you do it, the better you get at ignoring it," George laughed. "This show is my best option. If I didn't work here, I'd have to go to the poor farm or an asylum."

"Have you tried getting help for your condition? You could go see Dr. Harlow at the Medical College."

"Huh," chuffed George, "Wouldn't that be something?"

"I'll write a letter of introduction for you," I urged.

"Very kind. However, I've accepted my place. But you, Phineas.... When I look at you, I see a man with scars, but you can still walk and lift things; you have a strong back and strong hands. If I were you," George continued, "I'd join those crazy gold hunters going out west."

I was quiet as I thought about that. Finally, I glanced at him, grinning, "If you were the smallest man in the world, I could keep you in my pocket. We'd go adventuring. You'd be the brains, and I would be the brawn."

"That's why I like you, Gage, even with half a brain, you still have a healthy sense of humor."

ꔷꔷꔷ

A few weeks later, I left Barnum's. I exhibited myself independently in other New England towns until I settled into a job at the Dartmouth Inn. It is only six miles from Lebanon.

It felt so good, returning to honorable work as a stable hand. My back and muscles ached pleasantly from mucking out stalls. My sleep wasn't troubled by dreams or memories of curiosity seekers.

Horses only care about their food, how well they are maintained, and how much exercise they get. At times, I missed being the biggest toad in the puddle, like I used to be on my railroad gang. For now, the stable work suited me. The animals were happy, and I'd found my own measure of it.

The head coachman started training me to drive teams. It's more complicated than pulling a plow through the field, but a known voice, an understanding of personalities, and physical abilities go a long way toward getting it right. The main thing I had to learn was the feel of multiple straps laced through my fingers. There's a set for each pair of horses. Strap movements correspond with commands. After a while, I got good enough to do fill-in work.

I made deliveries with two and four horse teams, eventually taking passengers short distances once my driving skills improved.

I lived quietly at Dartmouth, keeping company with the animals, saving nearly every cent. I had close to three thousand dollars saved.

I went home to visit whenever I had time off. Our entertainment, then, was listening to Phoebe's letters. Her fiancé, David Shattuck, had gone out west last year. He described San Francisco and reported on his accomplishments. He kept saying that he'd be sending for Phoebe soon.

I kept wondering why not make a family adventure of it?

"The farms are in the capable hands of my brothers," I said to my parents. "Let's go, the four of us, and make a fresh start. I have plenty of money to get us there."

After we decided to go, I remembered George's comment about the crazy gold hunters. I wrote to him with our news.

I had a letter from his new wife before we left. Oh, what was her name? My thoughts turned dark. I detest having a mind that behaves like a sieve!

Gripping the ship's rail with both hands, I yelled, "It doesn't matter!"

George's wife... George's wife... I searched the empty corridors of my memory. She was the fat lady with a full beard... It made me laugh imagining tiny George with that large woman. Her name is Hester! There it was! I smiled triumphantly. Hester had written to tell me that they'd had a child; a perfectly healthy baby boy.

The thought of George and Hester's child brought Caroline to mind. When I think about her, my insides get agitated. In better times, we dreamed of our children. I hadn't realized how fortunate I was when I was just a man, with a girl, working for our future.

Longing and loss shoot through my heart, searing me. I blink back tears. Viewing undulating ocean swells through distorted vision doesn't help my mood or my wily guts!

One Sunday afternoon – years ago in Lebanon Caroline and me wandered off by ourselves, walking over the hill to a peaceful meadow, out of sight of the picnic and games. Caroline discovered a patch of Quaker Ladies flowers, tiny things with four white petals and a sunny center.

We set to work picking some when she asks me how many children I think we'll have.

"Coming from a large family," I said, "I think I'd like not so many that the middle ones get forgotten in the pack."

She giggled saying she agreed. I chose a flower, twirling it by its stem, sniffing its delicate perfume, "What would you name our first born?" I wanted to know. I reached over, plucking the pins from her hair, watching it tumble over her shoulders. She looks like she used to when she was a girl. Her smile sets my heart a flutter.

Her eyes sparkle, "I think I should like to name her, Susan."

"Susan!" I was surprised. "You are wishing for a girl first?"

"Yes, silly, girls are a great help around the home. She will watch the other little ones when I am laboring with the next."

"Come here," I said. She leaned toward me. I embed the flower stem in her loose hair. "Here's to the first," I say, kissing her.

For every child we named, I added a flower, following it with a kiss. We'd be breeding like rabbits if the Quaker Ladies were a prediction of our fate!

Before we started back, a gnat flew into my eye—the left one. The hurt that the tiny bug caused was out of proportion to its size. Caroline sat me down. While pulling my lower lid away, she dabbed with a corner of her handkerchief.

"For such a big, handsome man you yowl and complain like a baby," she observed with good humor.

When she'd gotten the critter out, she wiped at the tears running down my face, kissing the injured eye, then the other one for good measure. I had to thank her for her kind and gentle services... It is hard to stop thanking her! But a gentleman doesn't keep pestering a lady once she's called a halt.

Having Caroline to myself for that space of time, I was itching to finish saving for our farm and for us to be married! The need for money was what had sent me up Cavendish way.

A chilly wind crawling beneath my jacket brings me back to my place and time. Looking over the Atlantic waters, my mind conjures up my beloved. She stands beside me, her elbows on the deck rail. She leans into the wind. Her eyes are closed, but she is wearing a broad smile. "Every day is a new adventure!" she exclaims.

Turning toward me, her long, loose hair, behaves like autumn grass overcome by a dust devil. The Quaker Lady blossoms that I placed there come away, pelting my face with such force that they sting like blasting rubble.

My stomach is tight and sour, jumpy. Saliva, like hot water condensing along the sides of a glass pot, seeps into my mouth, filling the crevices below my tongue.

It occurs to me, with finality, that I will never be a father, now. That dream is as dead as my relationship with Caroline.

I hug the rail, opening my mouth, letting my guts erupt.

ПŊŊ

As the weeks on board the Witch of the Wave progress, I spent most of my time huddled on the mattress in my room. I refused attempts that my parents and sister made to get me to eat. Whenever I tried, even the crackers and water came right back up. I may end up as frail as George by the end of this torturous month-long voyage!

When I venture out, the other passengers know to avoid me. My foul temperament and disregard for social niceties send them scurrying in every direction. I don't much care.

Phoebe has said that my infirmity saves me from worrying over the boat sinking in the stormy seas—she may be right, I hardly notice when the ship bucks and leans.

My seasickness isn't the worst part of the trip. Sleep is. I fight it with every inch of my will. Reading can stave it off, but only when my stomach cooperates. I plead with my parents and Phoebe to read aloud to me after dark.

I shout at them when they refuse. Father is so tired of my behavior that he abandoned our room. He's boarding with Mother and Phebes.

რრრ

The nightmare is why I fight sleep. In it, I stand balanced on a piling in the middle of a lake. It is a beautiful day. The sun is shining. Birds are singing. Stretching out on either side of me are pilings going in both directions. I can effortlessly hop to the next one in the line.

In this strange landscape, I can see out of both of my eyes.

A breeze picks up across the water, pimpling my skin. Sand, blowing from east to west, pelts me, scratching my eyes. Turning my back to the wind, I begin jumping from pier to pier. Each footfall sounds, not of leather on wood, but of metal on stone.

Daylight is fading. The piers are growing farther apart. I have to balance, propelling my arms to gain enough momentum to make it to the next one. As I land, I hear the ring of iron and feel the tremble of an earthquake. I can see the shore isn't getting any closer. I've never been afraid of heights, and I am a strong swimmer, but something about falling in *this* water strikes terror into my heart.

Something big is down there, rippling the surface as it swims by, brushing against the piers. I begin to shiver, my breath hitches, in short, desperate gasps.

"Help!" I scream. The sound is carried away in echoing rings. Then it returns, blasting against my ear like a gun shot. Surprised, I lose my balance, swinging my arms in wild arcs. "Noooo!"

I'm falling! I tense, preparing for a fight. With a splash, the freezing water immobilizes me. For an awful moment, I am petrified, until the thing rams into me. It slams into my face with a blow like the full force swing of a baseball bat. My head whips back; I am tumbling, end over end, through the icy water.

Unable to hold my breath, I surrender to the urge to breathe. A mouthful of water sends a new wave of fear coursing through me. Frantically, I claw with arms and legs. I'm taking in water. When I stop struggling, my body sinks, gently. The light is growing dim, and I finally know peace.

Bubbles churn from below, surrounding me, clinging to my clothes, tickling my skin. Something grabs me, squeezing my arms against my chest and upper thighs. Together, the thing and I, rocket upward, breaking the surface.

Now, we are flying. I see the beach from far away, a tiny crescent outlined in blue. It is getting larger, racing toward me with frightful velocity.

The collision is sudden, abrupt, and crushing. Stunned, all I can do is blink and wonder if I have died.

Something soft and gelatin-like fills my nose and mouth. Gagging, I spit, pushing at it with my tongue. I can, finally, take a grateful breath.

My arms and legs still won't move; are they broken? I notice that the sun is getting warmer, uncomfortable, hot as I lay on the beach. Sweat gathers on my brow, dripping into my eyes, stinging, turning my vision cloudy.

Blinking, I see a girl standing at the edge of the forest. She walks toward me, a hand extended. Caroline! It's Caroline! A tiny blossom of hope blooms in my chest. When I would have called to her, I discover that my mouth is full again. This time it tastes of salt and feels like glass. Retching, I see that it is blood.

Broken and unable to move, I whimper. When my vision clears, Caroline is gone. In her place stands hundreds, or maybe thousands of crabs. Fist sized things, in a variety of blues and grays. With pinchers raised, they open and snap shut, in unison, like soldiers on a battle line.

Their tiny, unblinking eyes glare at me. At that moment, I understand what they want. At some unspoken command, they advance. My neck bulges with the force of my screams.

"No! No!" I yell, struggling. On some level, I am aware that my limbs are working, but I still feel trapped.

A soft hand and a quiet voice speaks to me. "It's a dream, Dear Heart. It's not real. Come out of it, Love," my mother croons. "Have a sip of water."

"No water!" I open my eyes, scuttling across the mattress. I blink slowly, becoming aware of the soft candle light and my mother perched there. She is wearing a dressing gown, her long braid trails down the side of her shoulder. She looks heavyhearted and tired. I swallow loudly, "I did it again, didn't I?" I yammer.

"It's alright; we'll get through this."

"Mama," I run a hand through my hair. It is damp, tangled, full of knots. My voice is plaintive, "I feel sick, and I can't sleep."

Patting her lap, Mother coaxes me to approach, "It's alright Phin, Phin, Mama's here."

Crawling over, I lay my head in her lap, allowing her gentle stroke to soothe me.

Phoebe

Tropics 1852

The captain says that we are about to enter the Bahamas. The air is noticeably warmer and heavier. It has a perfume in it that I've never known before.

I imagine my David in this place, smelling the same sweet aroma. Was he friendly with the sailors or keep to himself? We grew up, neighbors, in the same county, seeing the same sights, knowing the same people.

Since David left last year, his experiences have been very different. I can tell by his letters that he's changed. I hope the 'old' David is recognizable when we arrive in Yerba Buena. Mother says that my worries are unfounded. If David had changed so much, he would not have sent for me.

"Mrs. David Shattuck." That is how people will know me in San Francisco. I must not forget that this voyage is turning me into a world traveler too.

Phoebe unfolded one of David's letters. In block letters, he described crossing the isthmus. "We proceeded on canoes rowed by natives into a land so foreign it seemed like a fairytale. Hooting monkeys and brightly colored parrots completed the scene."

Phoebe brought the paper to her nose. Inhaling, she closed her eyes. "It's been so long, David," she whispered, "I can't remember what you smell like."

Carefully, she refolded the letter.

On board this ship, it feels as if service bells ring for me without end. I know that I am supposed to be a good and dutiful daughter and sister, but I am worried that my temper will show. If my true feelings came out, I would be a disgrace.

An artist on board who sketches botanicals showed me drawings of the flowers and plants we will see once we land. He's been teaching me watercolor techniques.

When I am painting, there is a small measure of deference for my time. People look over my shoulder to see if I am finished before asking me to empty a sick pan or go read to my brother.

On the farm, I could find places to be alone; collecting eggs, picking berries, chasing down escaped pigs or running errands for Mother. No one noticed if I sat by the creek, or climbed a tree.

Phoebe's stomach growled. As she began packing her paints and brushes away, she thought about the meal she was about to eat.

The food served in our class is tasteless but passable; it's not spoilt or infested with vermin. I've seen what goes down to steerage class. It's slop that I wouldn't feed my pigs. It is not surprising that they are in such ill health.

When the steerage passengers are allowed on deck, they look as bad as Phineas. The ship's physician says that cholera is rampant down there. I wish I could blot out the images of the children who've died. Their bodies wrapped in cloth and twine like Christmas gifts, sliding beneath the waves of an angry sea. The desolate cries of their mothers ringing in my ears.

I feel guilty that my bright hopes for the future can be conjured up by reading David's letters while the dreams of those poor mothers sink to the bottom of the ocean. Did Mother have those feelings when Phineas was sick?

We have Phineas to thank for our second-class accommodations. If Father hadn't accepted his money, we would have been down on the lower decks. Phin's seasickness would have been much worse had he been housed on a bunk, in the dark, without fresh air. Maybe some of us would have been buried at sea by now.

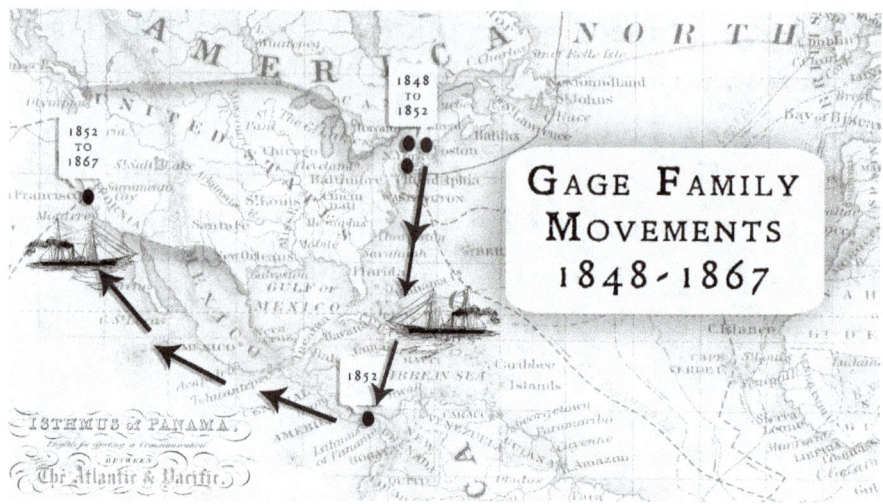

GAGE FAMILY MOVEMENTS 1848-1867

Eastern Panama: Isthmus Crossing 1852

Because the cove near Chagres is shallow, the Witch of the Wave laid anchor a mile out. Disembarkation took hours. Small row boats ferried passengers, cargo, and luggage to shore.

The Gage family opted to wait for a later row-boat rather than fighting against the crush of those racing to land. Phineas, leaned against the ship's rail watching the activity. "I've been imprisoned in this floating torture chamber for weeks. And, now, when we are so close to relief, you want to delay!" He complained bitterly. "I should have gone on the first boat. At least I could have waited on dry land!"

"Phineas, stop this behavior!" Jesse Gage reproached his eldest son.

"I am plenty annoyed, Father! I paid for most of this trip; I should have been consulted about how we ended it."

"Ladies," Jesse addressed his wife and daughter, "if you

will excuse us." Grasping Phineas by his elbow, Jesse escorted his son to the ship's aft.

Embarrassed, the women looked in the opposite direction.

Mr. McGill approached, "I couldn't help over hearing your son's complaints. I assure you that you will be in no danger of missing a guide for hire." While McGill spoke, his eyes followed the men. "In fact," he stated, "the quality guides prefer to work for clients who show a little patience."

James smiled at Hannah and Phoebe. They'd become well acquainted during the month-long voyage. "Please excuse my forwardness, but your son has suffered during the crossing. Once he's on land again, he'll recover quickly, I think."

"I do hope so!" Hannah replied.

Over McGill's shoulder, the women saw, with dismay, Phineas pulling his arm free. He stomped back toward them; they could tell that his temper hadn't abated.

"Speaking the language will be helpful on this next leg of your trip," McGill continued. "Do any of you speak Spanish?"

"In New York City, I heard," Phineas interrupted, "that the language barrier won't be a problem as long as we stay on the main route to Panama City."

"That may be true," McGill agreed complacently, "if you are fortunate enough to avoid the bandits. I assure you, they will not speak English."

"Jesse!" Hannah looked to her husband, who had also rejoined the group, "what are we to do?" She nodded in Phoebe's direction.

"Not to worry, Mother," Phineas supplied, "I've plenty of experience fighting off riff raff, plus we have the knives and guns that I bought for us."

Frowning, Hannah and Jesse regarded their son as if he had grown horns.

"If I may…." McGill said, "Traveling in small groups affords greater safety. I'm on my way to Chili but will be making a stop in Panama City. There's room in my party if you wish to join us."

"Thank you, Sir!" Jesse Gage smiled. He reached out, shaking James McGill's hand. "If you can put up with us, we'd be glad to accept."

ﬡﬡﬡ

Immediately upon landing, the voyagers experienced a wobbly sensation. It felt like the earth was moving like the ship.

Grasping objects to steady himself, Jesse exclaimed, "I can't walk a straight line!"

"Now you know what it seasickness is like, Father," Phineas shouted. He smiled broadly, "I feel better than fine for a change!"

"It is disembarkation sickness," Mr. McGill chuckled. "Give it time. Do some brisk exercise. You'll have your land legs before you know it."

James McGill led his party through the throng of natives and blacks, at the muddy edge of the bay, clamoring to sell items or haul luggage.

He took them to a small, out-of-the-way establishment. It was rudimentary but clean, a distance from the town where foreigners from every continent were shouting, drinking, and fighting. A wide outdoor veranda felt spacious, peaceful, and grand after the cramped conditions aboard the Witch.

The veranda was where the proprietors served a simple evening meal of polo con pepitas, freshly made corn tortillas served with citrus and cheese. The weary travelers ate sparingly; their stomachs were still tender. Phineas, however, consumed his food as if he was trying to make up for months of starvation.

Phoebe listened to her parents commenting how fortunate they were to have befriended James McGill; she watched the topic of their conversation eyeing her brother through the smoke of his after supper cigar.

ﬡﬡﬡ

As the sun was just beginning to lighten the horizon, frantic screams awoke Phoebe and Hannah from an exhausted slumber. It was Phineas! Throwing off their covers, they didn't bother with footwear or robes. Racing down the hall to the men's area, they saw Phineas crouched in a corner covering his ears, stammering, "Make it stop!"

Jesse and the rest of the men crowded around.
Phoebe was the first to notice a sound booming in the
distance. "What is that?"

Mr. McGill translated the question to the proprietor who
stood in the doorway, looking anxious.

"He says that they are building a roadway for the iron
horse up north," McGill repeated. "The explosions are
breaking through the hard rock."

"Good thinking, Daughter!" said Jesse. "My son's
injuries are from a blasting accident at home."

With each successive explosion, Phineas jumped, his
eyes wild, he rolled himself into a tight ball, rocking to
and fro. "Make it stop!" his screams unsettled the entire
household.

Finally, Jesse turned to his wife and daughter. "We must
leave. Ask McGill where we should go."

Packing their belongings with haste, the family prepared
to move. Phoebe and Hannah mounted their horses.

Before him on the saddle, Jesse held his grown son as
one would a small, terrified child. They followed one of
Mr. McGill's men to the next town, over a rise, where the
terrain might offer relief from the blasting.

Phoebe

Chagres River 1852

We rejoined Mr. McGill. Three of his men were running a mule train over land. Their journey would take three days longer than ours. They invited Phineas to join them. He agreed on the spot.

Mother argued with him, "You can't go off into the wilds without someone watching over you!"

"I'm a grown man, Mother. I survived in Boston and New York; I am capable of managing here."

"But you were so ill on the ship, and the blasting...."

Phineas paused as if searching for the right words, "These fellows have been around me since we started this trip. They know about my head. They've already seen the worst of me. I can help with the animals. I cannot—will not—get on another boat! Not even a small one."

Mother looked to father. He shrugged. "Phin's right, Hannah, he is a grown man. He will make his own decisions."

ꟿꟿꟿ

I know it's dreadful, but I was glad to see Phineas go! I love my brother, but the strain of having him around is never more evident than when he is absent.

A downpour soaked us as we waved goodbye. My parents ran for cover. I watched Thad, Oliver, and Paul pull down their hats and button their rain coats. Phineas, riding behind them, opened his mouth to catch the rain, smiling broadly, he waved back at me until he was out of sight.

By the time we were ready to depart, the sun was out again, bright and boiling.

The natives call their canoes, cayucas. Whites refer to them as bungos. Made of a single large, hollowed-out log, they are long, twenty-five feet or so, but narrow. Only three persons can sit abreast. Each bungo carries four to six passengers with three boatmen. Palm leaf or canvas canopies provide shade.

Mother was still unhappy with father when we boarded our bungo in the flotilla that would traverse the Lago Gatun. Refusing to speak to him, she was swiping at tears.

It took three days to travel up the river to Las Cruces. Our guides, through Mr. McGill, cautioned us to beware of snakes and certain insects.

Once again, we were grateful for being taken under Mr. McGill's wing. Bungos crowded the river going in both directions. The shores were so dense with foliage and snags; there would have been no way to land. We passed small, settlements with one or two canvas roofed buildings, crowded with foul tempered travelers and overburdened natives attempting to serve them.

Mr. McGill's guides had their own camp spots located a distance from the assemblages. The lean-tos were simple, but at least they were dry, and we had plenty to eat.

When we made camp on shore, Mother was anxious when I wanted to wander. I assured her that I'd be okay carrying my knife and gun with me.

When I brought back overflowing bags of fruit, her fears simmered down.

The watercolor hobby that I'd learned aboard

the Witch continued to be interesting in the Panamanian jungle. Wherever I went, I carried a small art pad and a simple collection of paints.

Spider monkeys are my subject of study. I could watch their antics all day. I always wish that I could get close enough to touch one.

I was off chasing my little darlings and searching for fruit one day when I heard awful screams. I am not a monkey, but I understood that their cries meant that something was seriously wrong. The wise thing to do would have been to return to camp. That is not what I did. I charged through the thick vegetation in a rush to see who was hurt and what I could do to help.

The shrieks grew louder as I got closer. Howler monkeys were going off like fire alarm bells; parrots were squawking and taking flight. I entered a clearing at the edge of a small tributary. On the opposite bank, I saw a life and death drama unfolding.

In an overhanging tree branch, a band of six or seven Spider monkeys was frantically jumping from perch to perch chattering and looking below. One was whimpering while another clutched it like a mother comforting a frightened child.

On the ground, was the largest snake I have ever seen! It was longer than I am tall and must have outweighed me by at least twice. I wasn't afraid because it was busy. It was eating one of the Spider monkeys.

Maybe the little dear had slipped or fallen, or the rope-like beast had been stalking it in the tree, but the poor thing was up to its armpits inside the snake's mouth. Most horrifying of all was that it wasn't dead. I could hear its weakening cries as it beat tiny fists about the reptile's snout.

With the snake's next spasmodic bite, the monkey's arms were immobilized. It ceased struggling. It lay there passively, looking up at its family. Then it squeezed its eyes closed. To me, it looked like he had said his goodbyes. When the snake took another measure, the monkey opened his eyes, meeting mine across the water.

My knees stopped supporting me; I sunk into the soft mud, keeping my gaze locked with the monkey's until the snake's mouth blocked even that.

The jungle returned to its twittering rhythms of sound, the band of Spider monkeys silently moved on, but the snake, with a monkey-sized bump along its length, remained. Its head, raised up, bobbling from side to side. Its forked tongue tasted the air. It knew I was there!

For the first time since the ordeal started, I was afraid. But I could not go without recording the extraordinary sight. With fumbling fingers, I pulled out my art supplies. My mouth was so dry I didn't have enough spit to wet the bristles. I leaned toward the river with my brush in hand.

The monster, keeping its unflinching eyes on me, lowered its head to the water's edge too. I felt as if I were gazing into an enchanted mirror. Monster and mistress matching movements. When my bristles dipped into the wet, the thing froze. It remained unmoving while I painted hastily. With my last stroke, it surged into the water, barely making a sound.

I sprang to my feet, running back to camp as if the thing had grown legs.

Everyone was eager to hear about my adventure, except for Mother. Without exception, they all wanted to look at my painting. Mr. McGill told us that the guide called the snake an anaconda.

Though it was late, and the camp was partially set-up, those who were most disturbed by my serpent encounter wanted to pack up and move. Mr. McGill said, 'no,' but he was gracious enough to post guards around the perimeter.

I missed Phineas. If he were here, he'd have encouraged me to make mischief with him— sounds and rustles that would further aggravate Mother and the others. I don't know if the guards or pistols would have deterred him.

Las Cruces was another intriguing city. Like all the others we visited, I could see it was a sleepy village that had transformed. Gold seekers and outsiders turned it into a place of peril.

Instead of spending the night, we loaded our rented mule train, setting off on the last eighteen miles before reaching Panama City, only one more night of camping. I thought that traveling by road again would be a welcome change. But torrential rains, ankle deep mud, rocks to traverse, and the sticky heat of the jungle made it a test of endurance.

It took us a total of four days to travel sixty-three miles across the isthmus. For Phineas and the other fellows, going over land, through the jungle, it took seven. I felt sorry for him.

Panama City 1852

We reached Panama City, at last! Still following Mr. McGill, we lodged at the American Hotel. It had single cots stacked on top of each other like shelves. It also had a proper a roof, walls, clean blankets, and bathing facilities. A good bath and dry, clean clothes felt like a blessing from heaven.

Here, we would wait for Phineas and the steamship that would take us to San Francisco.

The place was packed with travelers waiting for ships. Many of them didn't have tickets for the trip up north; they weren't having much luck obtaining them. Flaring tempers and sour moods were felt everywhere. Sickness was rampant; there were not enough people to nurse the ill. I heard stories of men dying here; their relatives back home never knowing what happened to them.

I tried not to be overly fretful about Mother and father suffering from diarrhea. Our hotel was clean, and I was keeping a close eye on them.

One afternoon, while they were sleeping, I joined the hotel owner's daughter on her daily chores.

In Conception's company, I helped take clothing to the river. Native women sat on the ground with flat wooden bowls, scrubbing fabric. If something needed a more thorough cleaning, they twisted it into a roll, beating it against rocks.

Washing wasn't that different no matter where you lived, I thought. The people, however, were very different. The women were dark skinned and dark haired. Many of the children wore no clothes. Everyone, including the little ones, smoked cigars.

Conception approached the women who did the washing for the hotel. Their dresses were decorated with lace and frills. They wore brightly colored scarves and shallow Panama hats with wide brims.

Noticing my interest in the cigars, Conception asked the women if we could have one. Accepting it, she lit it, taking a long drag. Smiling with encouragement, she held it out to me.

Startled, my first instinct was to say, 'No.' But the women looked at me with such curiosity that I didn't want to offend. I tried it.

Doing what Conception had done, I put the cigar to my mouth, then inhaled. It was awful! It felt as if my throat turned to fire. I started coughing; I couldn't stop. I thought my lungs would burst.

The women laughed nervously. Conception patted my back. A washerwoman offered me a jug. Looking to Conception, I sent a silent question. She shrugged.

After the cigar, I should have known that Conception was no friend. I accepted the jug with a nod. Taking a drink, another element of fire burned its way to my belly. What had I done to offend them? The hateful liquid burned as much on its second journey through my system. On my knees on the ground, I spit between coughing spasms, wondering if I would make it back to the hotel.

The eldest woman in the group brought me a cup of water. She rubbed my arm in a concerned, motherly way. Turning to Conception, she shouted words that sounded angry. The woman draped her green and purple scarf over my shoulders, "For you," she said, then, "come."

She led me down a path to a clearing. Conception followed at a safe distance. Two little girls sat playing with a branch of leaves and a furry doll. It had wiry hair, very long limbs, and sharp curved claws.

When it slowly turned its head, I could see that it was an animal! Big black eyes blinked. Under a blunt hairless nose, its mouth shaped into a smile.

"What is that?" I squatted down next to the little girl. My voice sounded brittle.

The mother smiled. "Perezoso," she pronounced slowly and distinctly so that I could try it. Once I had done so, the mother spoke to her daughter, gesturing at me. As the little girl stood, she unhooked the claws. Leaning over, she held out the animal's arms so that they were reaching for me.

Not able to resist, I lifted the Perezoso like a baby. The hind legs followed until I bore its full weight. It clung to me tightly, almost painfully. I stroked it. It wasn't soft like I imagined, but stiff and coarse like a hair brush. I crooned softly and rocked; it gradually relaxed. We gazed lovingly into each other's eyes.

The little girl brought over a large orange and red hibiscus flower. She held it up.

"Thank you," I replied, accepting the gift, raising it to my nose.

The Perezoso looked interested. "You want a smell too?" I lowered the flower. A hooked claw/hand over my wrist pulled it down. When the flower was close enough, the animal took a bite, chewing and smiling as if it was savoring every flavor. I burst out in surprised laughter. The women and little girls laughed with me. This sound was not mean spirited, but joyful.

When Conception indicated that it was time to go, I carefully returned the precious creature (I would later learn that it was a two-toed sloth) to its keeper. "Gracias!" I called happily, saying goodbye.

On the footpath back to town, I wondered if the onslaught of foreign travelers had changed Conception, turning her malicious, or if she had always been that way.

When I recognized my way back to the Hotel, I left her. I went to the beach looking for iguanas on the rocks to paint.

Sometime later, I was startled when a heavy hand fell on my shoulder, "They make pretty pictures, but they taste even better!"

"Phin!" I dropped everything, jumping to my

feet. I threw myself into his arms. "When did you get back?"

"Just now," he smiled. "I saw Mr. McGill over at the livery stables. He told me where to find you all. I was taking the scenic route along the beach."

Leaning back, I traced a finger along his smooth jawline, "You shaved, and you've cut your hair. You look handsome! It feels like forever since I've seen you."

"It's only been a few days," he chuckled good naturedly. He seemed more relaxed than I'd seen him in a very long time. He wasn't wearing his hat or hiding his face.

"There's much to tell, Phoebe," Phineas bent down to gather my paints, brush, and pad. He dropped his arm over my shoulder. "Where'd you get this thing?" he indicated the scarf.

"It was a gift from a woman down by the river."

"Another souvenir to show David."

"I can see that you are bursting with news...tell me."

Leading me back toward town, he said, "Let's say hello to Mother and Father first."

I told him about our parent s illness, the anaconda, smoking, drinking and about the Perezoso while we walked the three blocks to the hotel.

Mother and Father were so happy to see him. They were feeling much better.

Our meal that evening was a celebration. It was a pleasure seeing Phineas with his three traveling companions. They'd become friends. I could, almost, imagine that Phin's accident had never happened.

ריריר

A Fandango was being performed in the town square that night. The guests from the American Hotel walked together to the event. Street vendors, cooking Comida de feria, Arroz frito, and chorizo on a stick sent tantalizing aromas through the air.

I tied my new scarf around my waist; it draped down over my skirt, adding a splash of color. "I hope we get to dance," I said to Henry Trevitt, the newest member of our group.

"If you make eye contact with the performers, they might invite you to join," he replied grinning.

Henry's uncle was the American Consul in Valparaiso. Having graduated recently from university in the states, Henry came down to help Mr. McGill and company develop a coach line in his uncle's territory.

Henry and Phineas behaved like friends who'd known each other all their lives.

We spent the evening chatting and watching the show. When it was over, the performers walked through the audience. I made eye contact as Henry had suggested. I was the first one chosen!

The musicians played with increased vigor as the dancers taught us the steps. Everyone laughed and cheered.

಄಄಄

It was dark when the Gage family strolled back to the hotel. Phineas lent his arm to his mother; Phoebe tucked her hand into her father's elbow. "That was unforgettable, Father."

"Indeed, we'll have a lot to say when we next write to your brothers and sister."

She smiled, "Phineas is getting along with the fellows."

"He's better than I've seen him in a long time."

When they said their goodnights, Phoebe could see that

her parents did not approve of Phineas smoking cigars and playing cards with the men, but she also noticed that they kept their feelings to themselves.

Seeing her brother at ease made Phoebe wish that Phineas had not pushed Caroline away, she should be on this adventure with them.

ಬಬಬ

Phineas's way with animals, especially horses, had been valuable on the overland trip. McGill's boys invited him to join them while they inspected a shipment of horses that had arrived in port.

"Come with us, Phoebe!" Phineas urged. "It will do you good to see some quality horseflesh."

He and the men were preparing to depart.

"Really?" she enthused. "Shall I tell Mother and Father that we'll be gone all day?"

When Phineas opened his mouth to say that the trip wouldn't take that long, he caught the look on her face. Smiling, he nodded.

ಬಬಬ

Phoebe was excited to see San Francisco and her fiancé, but she'd fallen in love with Panama. She liked its heat, the exotic animals, and the colorful, shabby cities with delicious food.

Since they'd be departing any day, Phoebe was eager to see a few more sights.

She tuned-out the men's talk of horse breeds, transcontinental transportation, and Concord coaches. Instead, Pheobe memorized the locations she wanted to return to with Phineas.

He'd been busy every day since his arrival with Henry and Mr. McGill. He promised that they'd spend the afternoon together today.

She smelled the stock yard before it came into view. Pens housing animals that traveled around the Horn looked like a checkerboard.

"This way," Mr. McGill ushered her quickly toward the horses. His attempt to shield Pheobe from some of the unsavory sights was not entirely successful. She heard plaintive cries and glimpsed half-starved, suffering cattle in the enclosures.

The livery had large doors and windows that let in light and sea breezes. It was tidy. Hay lining the stalls was sweet and clean. The horses nickered greetings, gladly accepting the attention they received.

"It's been weeks since they've stretched their legs. My glossy new coaches are stored just across the way. Is anyone ready for a drive?"

At Phin and Phoebe's enthusiastic response, Thad, Oliver, Paul and Mr. McGill set to work laying out tack and outfitting the six-horse team. Phineas wasn't content to be a spectator. He joined in, commenting on the quality of the leather and the stable master's competence.

Phoebe caught Mr. McGill watching her brother. He

asked stabling questions. As Phin prattled out answers, non-stop, he didn't seem to notice the subtle interactions between McGill and his men.

The horse's coats quivered. They snorted and stomped. Walking behind them, Paul held the reins, giving the command to move. The men walked on either side as they progressed toward the carriage house.

Phoebe and Henry oohed and aahed as the shiny conveyance rolled out into the sunlight. Henry complimented the detailing of the paint and leather upholstery.

The new rig with the horses attached was a magnificent sight. Mr. McGill clapped his approval. He asked Phoebe if she'd paint a few scenes that he could take with him to Valparaiso.

When all was ready, Mr. McGill gallantly held the coach door open, raising a hand to assist Phoebe as she stepped up. Mr. McGill and Henry joined her. She expected Phineas to follow, but he poked his head in, grinning widely, stating that he would ride up top.

The coach inched its way down the narrow streets. Pedestrians parted, making way; women and children smiled and waved. Phoebe waved back, feeling as if she were the queen of England.

On the outskirts of town, where the road widened, Mr. McGill leaned out the window, shouting to the driver, "Give them their heads, Mr. Martin!"

The coached lurched forward as horsepower kicked in. The occupants inside grabbed hold of something. Their ride jostled on its springs. They could hear the men on the roof cheering. With her free hand, Phoebe reached into her handbag to remove a handkerchief. She clamped it over the lower half of her face. Although the speed and rocking were invigorating, she didn't care for the dust.

After a good twenty minutes, the coach slowed, Oliver leaned over the side to speak to Mr. McGill. "Over the next rise, Sir is a small village. We thought we'd stop to water the horses."

"Good!" James shouted, "Tell the others that we'll do some handling tests."

ന ന ന

For the next several hours, the cluster of men watched, criticized, evaluated, and refined their horse and coach maneuvering skills.

As Phoebe painted scenes, Mr. McGill explained that his task was to commission and deliver coaches and horse teams to Valparaiso, Chili, over 3,000 miles to the south. Valparaiso was a port-of-call for east-west travelers who sailed around the Horn. The coach line would transport tourists around the city and to Santiago, the capital city, a must-see destination.

From atop the coach, Thad Martin held the reins aloft, gesturing toward Phineas, "Want to give it a go?"

"Hell yes!" he grinned, striding forward.

"Your brother is good with horses," Mr. McGill observed, watching the proceedings.

"He always has been. He took care of them on our farm and worked in the stables at the Dartmouth Inn."

"How is he at driving teams?"

Phoebe smiled, "We are about to find out." She watched as Thad made room for Phineas in the driver's seat.

Phoebe heard Thad give quiet instructions about threading the straps. "A good driver, never puts force on these, unless his animals are out of control. It's a cooperation between man and beast. Use your voice first then confirm it with light directions on the leads."

Phineas nodded but did not give the command for the team to move. Returning the reins to Thad, he said, "Don't go anywhere."

Phineas climbed back down then walked to each horse patting it, speaking softly. Stopping at the front two, he stroked their heads, blowing softly into their noses.

With fast motions of her brush, Phoebe painted Phineas nose to nose with the animals.

Phineas nodded before climbing back up. Smiling broadly, he said, "We're all ready now." Under Phin's hands, the team glided forward, making a smooth turn around the village.

"Care to take a spin, Lady, and Gentlemen?" Phineas asked, coming to a halt beside Phoebe, McGill, Henry and the others.

He delivered them to the town center so Phoebe and Henry could find lunch. They located a small rustic establishment where they ordered arrollado huasco and chapalele.

Oliver was driving when Phoebe and Henry came out into the street with baskets under their arms. "Mmm...mmm...mmmm that sure smells good," he commented. "What's for supper?"

Climbing aboard, Henry grinned. "It's pork rolls and potato bread. We also got some spicy tomato sauce— chancho en piedra."

Sitting under a large shade tree, they enjoyed their food and each other's company. Phineas was the first to finish.

He returned to the horses, bringing them water and rubbing them down.

On the way back to Panama City, Phoebe was pleased to see her brother winning the esteem of the other men.

ɲɲɲ

Later that afternoon, Phineas and Phoebe were on their own at the beach. They unlaced their shoes and peeled off their stockings. Phineas rolled up his pants; Phoebe hiked her skirt around her waist. They raced across the white sand and into the water, scooping it and splashing at each other. They laughed freely like children again.

Spying a small round object ahead, Phoebe ran over to pick it up. "Look, Phin, a sea urchin shell. It's perfect, not a piece is missing, good luck for us!"

"Phebes," Phineas grew serious. Holding her elbow, he steered her away from the water, "let's find some shade so that we can talk."

"You look so grim; you're frightening me."

"I've made a decision."

"Oh?"

"James offered me a place on his coach team, and I've accepted."

"Phineas," Phoebe lay a hand on his arm, her voice was relieved, "you don't mean that. You're always thinking of schemes, but they never last. We're going to San Francisco—together. You said you might try your hand at gold mining."

"I'm done with rocks and railroads. And I'm not stepping foot on another ship. If I make my way to San Francisco one of these days, maybe I'll start a coaching company there."

Phoebe was distressed, "You're not coming to my wedding?"

"I do regret that dear Phoebe," Phineas said slowly, "but you don't need me to live a happy life with David."

"But, Phin, I'll miss you!"

Phineas blinked rapidly. "I'll miss you too, Phebes and the whole family."

Phoebe inhaled deeply as if accepting his words. She stared quietly out over the water before asking, "How did you leave things with Caroline?"

"She didn't tell you?"

Phoebe shook her head.

Phineas faced seaward, also, as he summoned his words. "We parted as treasured friends," Phineas swallowed with difficulty. "I told her that I wanted her to be free to find a husband who could offer all of the things that I no longer can."

"Phineas! I thought that you would send for her once you settled in Alta California."

"Phoebe—" he looked at her with a pained expression. "You love me, and because of that you don't see me the way others do—"

"Caroline loves you too!"

"I don't want pity and compassion from a woman. Surely you can understand that?"

Pheobe shook her head looking bewildered.

"I'm not fit to be Caroline's husband," Phineas said. "I'm not fit to be a husband to any woman." With a serious expression, he considered his sister.

When he spoke next, it was with quiet dignity, "It is what it is, Phoebe, there is no going back, only forward. I did what was right by Caroline—and, now, I have to do what is right for me."

Phoebe's lips trembled, unshed tears rimmed her eyes, she nodded silently. Pushing her shoulders back and adjusting her spine, she took a breath. Forcing a smile, she regarded her brother. "I want what's best for you, Phin, if this is it, then I support you."

"There's my girl." Phineas smiled, affectionately rubbing and patting her hand, he gave it a firm squeeze.

ฌฌฌ

Phineas waved farewell from the docks when his sister and parents boarded the steamship bound for San Francisco.

He was excited about the turn his life had taken. In the company of his new friends, they prepared to drive five beautiful Concord Coaches three thousand miles to the south.

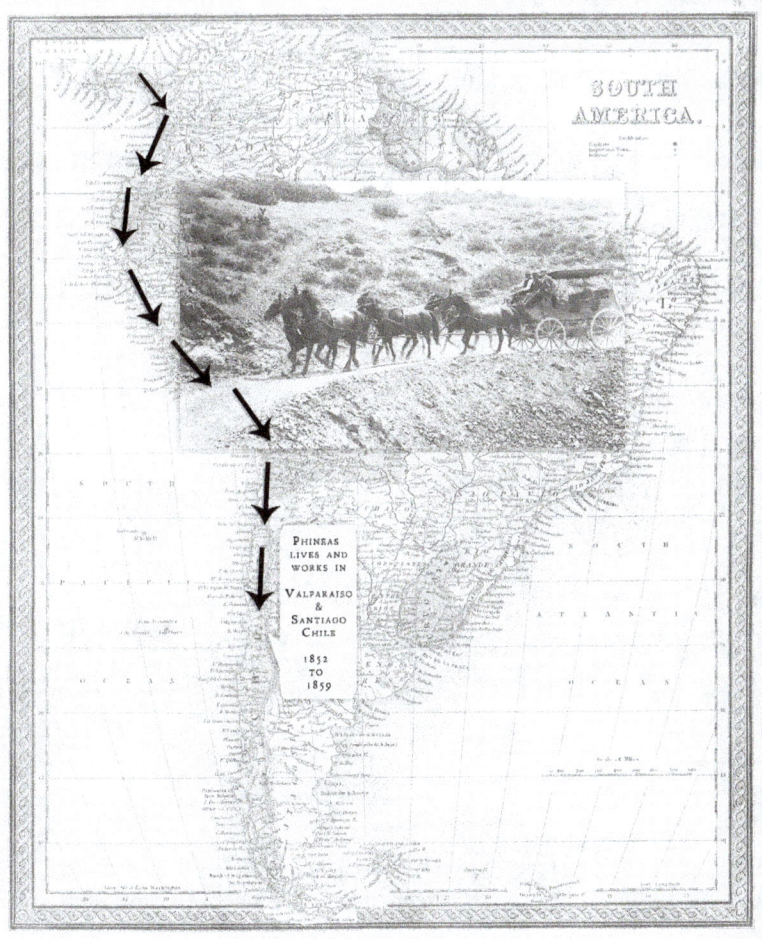

Not long after her arrival in San Francisco, Phoebe married David D. Shattuck. Five years later, she gave birth to their first child, Frank. When Phoebe saw her brother again, Frankie was two and a half years old.

San Francisco: July 1859

Eleven Years After the Accident

After suffering a series of illnesses, Phineas traveled to San Francisco to stay with his widowed mother. As it did the last time, the sea voyage wreaked havoc. Phineas arrived feeble, unsteady, foul mouthed, and mean tempered.

Once again, Hannah nursed her son back to health. While he recuperated, Phineas enjoyed the company of his mother, sister, and David. Getting acquainted with his young nephew was a delight.

Phineas had an endless supply of entertaining stories about his adventures as a coach driver in Chili. The family wasn't sure how much truth there was in those heroic tales.

רורות

One afternoon, sitting with Phoebe in her backyard, Phineas said, "So nice to be with you again, Phebes."

"I was heartbroken in Panama when I thought I might never see you again." She reached over, placing a hand on his arm.

"You've turned out to be a good wife and mother, Phoebe. David and his business have done well. You should all be proud."

"Thank you," Phoebe said remembering the feeling of awe she'd first felt when she stepped off the boat in San Francisco. It had been a metropolis compared to Panama.

She wondered if Phin had felt the same upon his arrival.

They sat in companionable silence for a while before Phineas asked, "Do you still write to Caroline?"

Without saying a word, Phoebe regarded him. She nodded cautiously.

"Did she marry?"

Phoebe nodded.

"Children?"

"Yes."

Phineas leaned back before asking, "Is she content with her life?"

Phoebe blinked rapidly. Her eyes glistened. "She says that she is. She asks about…."

Phineas shook his head vehemently. Their conversation died off as he scooted forward in his chair. Drawing in a breath through his nose, he braced his elbows on his knees. "I have a story for you."

"Oh? Is it like the ones that you tell Frankie?"

"No, this one doesn't involve heroes or bandits. This one is about love." Phineas settled back, extending his legs, crossing his ankles. He winked at her, making her smile.

Phineas

Yaimia

"Santiago, in some ways, is like Panama City, but it is much larger. Surrounded by the Andes mountains to the east and the Chilian Coastal Range to the west, it is the Capital city. It has a university, and schools for arts as well as a Museum of Natural History. A few of my passengers said that the architecture reminded them of Rome or Athens."

"They were building a large central park and major thoroughfares. The telegraph system was already running between there and Valparaiso. This is why James brought the coaches in. I too saw, right away, that was a smart investment."

"On our stage line, it was a three-day journey each way between Valparaiso and Santiago. The drivers and stable hands alternated between stops. When I was there for a week at a time, I'd drive for day visitors."

"One evening after I'd stabled and fed my team, a cowboy was in the stall next door grooming his prized steed, Dark Star. I listened to them, I liked how he talked, how she responded. I watched him removing long strands of hair from his curry comb, folding them into a pouch. When I asked him what he was doing, he told me his story."

Phineas adjusted in his seat, propping an ankle on his knee. Phoebe settled in to listen, closing her eyes as if preparing her imagination to create moving pictures.

"The Indians come down from the mountains to trade," the cowboy said.

"They followed the same roads that I drove, Phoebe," Phineas interjected. "The natives are short, thick of limb, dark haired and dark eyed. They keep to themselves, speaking to whites only when necessary.

"Skilled weavers are esteemed by the tribes," the cowboy continued. "Their fabrics and blankets represent their culture and are used to swop for things that they can't make. "

"When they come to Santiago, they place a blanket on the ground, displaying their wares. They wait patiently, smiling, and hoping that visitors walking by will notice."

"One day when I returned to where my horse, Star, was hitched, something spooked her. My hand was smashed between the post and her foreleg. I yelled. Star moved immediately, but the hand was torn and badly bruised."

"As I stood there holding it, watching the blood drip, a young woman approached. She spoke in her native tongue. I only knew a few words, but her meaning was clear."

"She held out a pure white cloth woven with intricate patterns; it was pure white, not a spot on it. She urged me to put my injured hand into it. I hesitated, not wanting to spoil such a thing of beauty. She acknowledged my reluctance with a curt nod, then reached out, gently taking my hand, wrapping it tightly. She pressed firmly until the bleeding stopped."

"Then she unwrapped it, glancing at my face. She might have been checking to see if I was feeling pain. After inspecting the wound, she raised her head, scanning the avenue, probably looking for a well. Not finding what she wanted, she started poking me in my middle. I was so startled to be touched this way by a woman that I jumped and laughed."

"I noticed her big doe-brown eyes were framed by thick lashes; her smooth skin was the color of coffee. Her mouth turned up in an indulgent smile. That was the moment that I first truly looked at her. She was a tiny thing, a deep earth knowledge radiated from her. We were from two different cultures, two different backgrounds, but we shared a connection."

"She pulled the flask that I carry out of my pocket. Opening it, she doused the hand. I screamed like a cat with a mangled tail."

"She continued holding the hand as she dug into a bag slung over her shoulder. Bringing out a pinch of dry powder, she sprinkled it over the injury. It stung almost as bad as my whiskey."

"Once she finished, she used the soiled cloth to wipe away the remaining blood, alcohol, and medicine. Urging me to follow her across the street to her little space along the walkway, she selected another long narrow cloth that she wrapped snuggly around my hand, neatly tucking in the edges."

"She refused payment or trade."

"When I returned to Star, I looked over at her as I climbed into the saddle. She was watching. We smiled, I raised my bandaged hand in farewell."

"I was surprised at how quickly my hand healed. Whenever I returned to Santiago, I went out of my way to ride by the Indian woman's roadside space. I brought friends and tourists to buy her wares. She worked eagerly to learn my language."

"Her name was Yaimia. Her mother was the master weaver in their village, but Yaimia was learning to weave too. She eyed Star with interest whenever we talked. "

"One day I asked her if she'd join me for a ride. It didn't take more than five minutes to wrap her blankets and cloths into a pack that she would take with her. I tied it over Star's rump, then lifted Yaimia onto the saddle in front of me."

"I believe that we fell in love that afternoon. She fit so perfectly in my arms. I never wanted to let her go."

"Yaimia, with her beautiful skin and trusting smile, never once noticed my scars."

Here, Phineas, coughed, interrupting the story, "I forgot to mention that the cowboy had a disfigured face." He waved at his own, "Like this one."

Phoebe opened her eyes, cocking her head. She wore a bemused expression. Her gaze searched every surface of her brother's countenance.

"Neither of us was invisible to each other anymore,' the cowboy had said."

"Yaimia approached me when she'd see me. She let me take her riding. Then one day, it was more than an afternoon adventure in the countryside. The sound of her laugh, the smell of her skin, the tastes of her mouth were something I craved daily. She became the most alluring woman in the world to me."

"I found us a hut at the edge of town where we lived as man and wife whenever we were in the city together. I was worried about Dark Star in that neighborhood, so I built a room for her in our house. It had a window she could poke her head through if she wanted to visit."

"Yaimia loved Dark Star as much as I did, she learned to groom her, saving the long tail hair for her mother."

"My sweet Yaimia's belly grew round. I wanted us to be married by a priest and to live in a proper house. But she refused, saying that her child would continue traveling with her and learn to sell cloth on the street."

"She could see that this made me unhappy, so she told me of her tribe's tattoos. 'We mark our bodies on special occasions—to remember,' she'd said. Yaimia asked me if I wanted her to make one for me. After much thought, I agreed."

"Over the course of several weeks, I lay on my back while she worked with her little needles and bottles of ink. She said that the design she'd chosen was Lukutuwe, the supreme being.

He was the first person with hands, feet, head, and heart. When she finished with me, Yaimia marked her thigh with the same design."

"I told Yaimia that I thought that our matching tattoos were like wedding rings. They were symbols showing that we were a family. She said it was true, that love bonded us, but that our family would never be like an Anglo family."

"I worried about Yaimia being on her own so much as her pregnancy progressed. What if she went into labor along the trail?

No one bothered her in Santiago, but once the baby was born, I wondered if she would suffer within the social structure of her tribe. When I voiced these concerns, she smiled brightly, kissing me, telling me that, "The Mapuche are not like the whites. We believe that all children belong with their mothers."

"The next time we saw each other, her infant was in a sling next to his mother, wrapped in a brightly colored cloth. I am a man brimming with machismo, but when Yaimia placed that tiny baby in my arms, I wept."

"She called him Pichi. It means 'small boy.' She said that, in her village, the man chooses the child's first name. I chose Del for him."

"Del Pichi grew like summer green beans; stretching toward the sun, grabbing everything and climbing. We did silly things to make him laugh."

"One day, after several weeks apart, Yaimia brought a little doll her mother had made from Dark Star's hair. In our home that night, she wove a tiny dress for it with our tattoo design on its belly. She put the dress on the doll and presented it to me proudly."

"It's Del Pichi, I exclaimed. She nodded, saying that it would keep me company when we were not together."

"The boy was healthy. His skin and eyes were lighter than his mother's. He crawled for a time but then decided he'd rather run. When he started speaking, it was in both our languages."

"Yaimia told me that her village was starting to have problems. The population of Santiago was growing.

There had been clashes between her people and others who wanted their ancestral lands."

"I asked her to join me, permanently, in Santiago, but Yaimia refused."

"A day came when Yaimia and Del Pichi didn't return. I waited with growing foreboding. I'd heard talk of the conflict with the Indians and the need to clean out the filth."

"I was afraid. We'd found a little piece of happiness, and I was frantic not to lose it."

"I never knew the location of her village. How could I have only known half of their lives—my half? Why didn't I ask to meet her people; her family? I rode into the bush searching for them every day for a full year. "

"Most of the Indians in the forest and in town would not speak to me. A few of them did. They said that Lukutuwe gives and Lukutuwe takes. To fight against it invites disaster."

Phineas stopped speaking. Phoebe leaned forward saying, "You can't stop there. Did he ever find his son?"

Phineas turned to look at his sister, wearing a faraway expression. Grimly, he continued, "I don't think he did.

But he gave me this." Phineas held up a crude doll made of hair, wearing a dress with a little design on the front.

"The cowboy said that someone who knew the story of Yiamia and Del Pichi should have it."

When Phineas did not continue, Phoebe straightened. "That's it? What happened to him? Why did he give it away? Phineas, that's not a good ending!"

"You're right," Phineas agreed. "It's messy, but it has a few good parts."

Phineas stood abruptly. As he tucked the doll back into his jacket, he said, "Mother might not agree, but I've regained the weight I lost at sea, and my energy is back. I thought I might ask David about work."

It took Phoebe a few moments to respond. She was distracted when she replied, "He knows most of the business men in town."

꒰꒰꒰

David did have a contact. It was on a farm down in Santa Clara. "The work will be similar to what we used to do in New Hampshire, digging up tree stumps and preparing fields for planting."

"It sounds like honest work," replied Phineas.

"The Johnsons provide room and board along with weekly pay."

"Even better!"

"Phineas, I have a request."

"Anything, David, just ask."

"Would you return to San Francisco often to help look after Mother Gage? She's getting on in years. Phoebe needs help, but she'll never ask."

൫൫൫

For half a year, the work on the farm went well. Phineas came back to stay with his mother every other weekend.

Hannah made lists of repairs and errands that she wanted Phineas to do while he was there. She said that her house hadn't been so well maintained since she and Jesse bought it.

On Sunday afternoons, David and Phoebe hosted large family suppers that included David's parents, siblings, nieces, and nephews. Hannah and Phineas enjoyed the walk over when the weather was balmy.

John, David's younger brother, came in from outside one afternoon, a grin still lingering on his face. He joined David who stood at a window watching the scene in the front yard. Phineas was pushing his niece in the swing, tossing balls for the dogs and regaling Frankie and the other boys with a lively story.

"He's telling them about the famous one-eyed cowboy from Santiago," John commented.

David nodded, clapping his brother on the back, "That's a good one."

"Do you think any of it is true?"

"With Phineas, you never know. But who cares? The children love it and, so does he."

Dinner: April 17, 1860

Eleven Years and Seven Months After the Accident

At dinner one night, later that summer when thunder clouds hung low over a city silenced by humidity and heat, John brought up the recent Indian massacre in Humboldt County.

Hundreds of Wiyot women, children, and elders were slaughtered by an unnamed group of white men. An anonymous letter published in the San Francisco Bulletin had referred to Eureka as Murdersville, saying that in the churches there, "The pulpit is silent, and the preachers say not a word."

Phoebe drew in a breath to speak when her brother spilled a full glass of water in her lap. "Phineas!" Phoebe cried, rising from her chair. When she turned to face him, she saw that his eyes were wide, staring in horror at the faces around the table, his mouth hung open in a grimace.

"What is it?" She leaned over, placing a hand along his face, "Are you thinking of the Indians from Santiago?"

His gaze locked with hers, he made an anguished moan, nodded twice, then his eyes rolled back.

"Something's wrong!" Phoebe shouted.

Phineas's body was stiff as if it had turned to wood. His neck arched. He bucked and shuddered. His hands were claw-like. They turned out at right angles; his feet did the same.

David raced over, "He's choking!"

"Check his throat!" David's father, Michael, commanded, "Ladies take the children away from here!"

The frightened women followed the directive. Phoebe and Hannah remained, clutching each other as if the force of their grasp could miraculously stop what was happening to Phineas.

As gently as possible, David lowered Phineas to the floor. His convulsions had ceased, but his body remained stiff, unyielding, his breathing labored.

"Send one of the children for the doctor!" Hannah yelled toward the other room.

"Make way everyone," David said. While Phoebe and Michael moved toppled chairs, clearing a path, David knelt, scooping Phineas in his arms like he would his little son, but Phineas weighed too much. Michael came forward and, together, they transported the inert man to a bed. Hannah followed, wringing her hands.

Phineas seized again. Michael retrieved a wooden spoon from the table, forcing it between Phineas's teeth. Two more convulsive fits came in short bursts. When they passed, Phineas seemed vacant. The pupil of his eye was visible, but he wasn't responsive.

Visibly shaken, Hannah and Phoebe were as pale as ghosts. David and his parents weren't much better.

Phineas fell into a peaceful sleep. When he woke, he gazed at everyone in the room, one after another. "Why are you all staring at me?"

The doctor arrived. He listened to Phineas's heart and

lungs; he inspected his eye and tongue. Phineas had no memory of what happened and no forewarning that anything out-of-the-ordinary would occur. "I feel alright," his voice was edgy.

Phoebe stayed with Phineas while the rest of the family joined the Doctor in the living room where he patiently listened as they gave him details that they recalled. Nodding as if he'd heard it before, he pronounced, "It was an epileptic seizure."

"Is it related to his accident? Will it happen again?" Hannah asked.

"There's no way to know," he replied. "We will have to watch and wait. If it reoccurs, come fetch me."

The slamming of a door startled them. Phoebe rushed in, flustered. "He's gone! Phin said he didn't believe it; he said he didn't know why we ganged up on him. He's in a state!"

The Doctor nodded, "Denial and anger are typical stages of processing after a traumatic event. He needs time to adjust, you all do."

David

Work: April 22, 1860

Phineas didn't return to the farm in Santa Clara. Instead, he asked me to find work for him in town. I did, but in every situation, Phin found something grievously wrong.

His accusations about his employers were bad enough on their own, but making them, loudly, in the store where customers overheard was inexcusable.

"The Copperfields are cheaters and crooks."

"That Clint MacIntosh starves cattle and kicks his dogs."

"Sadie Inverwall expected me to supply my own tools; she shorted my pay."

"Phineas, everyone can't be at fault." I complained, "You're damaging my reputation and burning all your bridges."

I could see by the murderous thunder clouds gathering in his expression that he didn't like hearing the truth. In a rage, he slammed a fist on a glass display top, shattering it, "It's not me, David!"

੫੫੫

Whenever Phineas didn't show up for supper, Mother Gage pleaded with me to search the taverns for him. If I found him falling-down drunk, it was easy to carry him home and dump him in his bed.

He'd be sick in the morning, leaving Mother Gage in relative peace.

It was more problematic if Phineas wasn't all the way gone. He reacted violently to being fetched. "You've turned into a lap dog, David Shattuck, taking orders from my mother and my sister!" Spittle flew from his mouth; he looked demonic. "Don't you have better things to do than to harass me?"

Biting my tongue, I hauled Phineas out of his seat. Then he threw glasses, knocked over chairs, and kicked. Fortunately, his reflexes were delayed and inaccurate. The barkeeps knew, by now, to send a bill for damages to my store.

On those nights, I could have punched him just to shut his mouth. But the Heavenly Father tells us to turn the other cheek. I owed my wife and mother-in-law more than beating their kin over wounded pride.

Not so long ago, Phineas gave a Spaniel pup to Frankie. A happier child, I've never seen. The dog's name is Roxanne.

Roxanne reminded me of Rolo, a hound pup Phineas had given me when I was Frankie's age. Phineas took us hunting, showing me how to wield a knife to clean birds and other small game. We built fires in the woods where we roasted our kill on sharpened sticks. I looked up to Phineas, then.

Before I lost my heart completely to Phoebe, my heart was thinking about Caroline. She was older, but I didn't care. If ever there was an angel who'd landed on earth, it was her. Pretty as a picture, kind, with a singing voice that brought tears to my eyes.

For Caroline, there was never anyone other than Phin. Something broke in her when he turned her away after his accident. *She'd be mighty disappointed to see what's become of him now.* I thought as I supported his heavy weight, dragging him along the sidewalk. *In spite of what my wife thinks, I believe he was right to spare her this.*

Phineas's behavior was going from bad to worse. He was progressively growing more erratic and angry. "I don't want you or little Frank around him anymore," I told Phoebe. "He could harm you or our unborn child. I'm worried about your mother too. If he keeps on this way, we'll have to commit him to the insane asylum."

"Heaven forbid!" Phoebe said, covering her heart with a fluttering hand, "I've heard that they sterilize every patient!"

"We have bigger problems than your brother's sex organs to worry about."

Seizure: May 18, 1860

Eleven Years and Eight Months After the Accident

Strange sounds coming from Phineas's room woke Hannah at 5:00 a.m.

Donning a robe and lighting a lamp, she hurried down the hallway, opening the door to his room. His leg stuck out from under the covers. Phineas was stiff and convulsing. His bed rattled against the wall.

"Phineas!" Hannah screamed. Terror filled her. Helplessly she called her son's name.

As the seizure continued, Hannah realized she needed help. She ran as fast as she could to David and Phoebe's, banging in desperation at the glass on their front door.

David

I heard mother's voice and rushed to answer in my bed rumpled state, "What's the matter, Mother Gage?"

"It's Phineas; he's seizing again! It's terrible, David! It's not stopping," her voice was shrill.

Two months had passed since Phineas seized at our house. I sympathized, it was a dreadful thing to watch. "Calm yourself; we'll help."

Phoebe, large in her seventh month of pregnancy approached, wide-eyed with worry. "David, go with Mother. I'll ask Mrs. Murry next door to sit with Frankie while I go to fetch the doctor."

Ꙩ Ꙩ Ꙩ

The doctor strapped Phineas's arms and legs to the bedposts. Once the patient's erratic movements were controlled, he tied rubber tubing around Phineas's forearm. Holding a bowl below his elbow, he lanced along a vein, opening it.

The bloodletting therapy didn't help. Phineas convulsed on and off through the day and into the next night. In between, he slept restlessly or moaned. His eye looked vacant.

My wife and mother-in-law remained with him in a tormented vigil.

"I didn't think anything could be worse than when he was in Cavendish, but this is," Phoebe exclaimed.

Mourning: May 21, 1860

Eleven Years, Eight Months, and Eight Days
After the Accident

When Phineas's statue-stiff, quaking body came to rest, Hannah folded his limp hands over his chest.

She stroked his cheek, "He looks like he's sleeping," she mused, "God has taken back what he let me borrow." Hannah leaned down, kissing him, "You were a good boy, Phineas."

David

Mother Gage's house took on a hushed silence as she and Phoebe prepared for mourning. Mother went to her linen closet for the crepe she used to cover the mirrors and shiny surfaces.

She tied a black ribbon to the front door.

Phoebe chose Phin's burial clothes. "I did this once before," she remembered. Phoebe's shoulders shook, there was nothing I could say or do except to hold her.

Together we worked at removing Phineas's drawers and nightshirt. I rolled the body onto its side, while Phoebe slipped her brother's arm out of a sleeve. "There's something in here," she hesitated as she pulled the nightshirt away."

I watched as she removed an object from a pocket. It was a dark, hairy thing, with a human shape. "What's that?" I asked.

Looking down, she said, "It's nothing. A souvenir from Chili." Phoebe put it away.

Hannah came in with a bowl of warm, lavender scented water. I left so the women could bathe him in private.

Mother and daughter didn't speak as they worked. Moving and handling the body; washing his hands, limbs, and feet, trimming his nails and combing his hair.

When they were ready to dress him, Phoebe called me back. I was holding Phineas's hands close to his knees as she and Mother Gage slipped a clean undershirt over his head. I heard my wife gasp.

"Phoebe?"

"Look!" she pointed to an area at the base of Phineas's back.

Mother Gage leaned over, "It's a tattoo," she whispered, "I wonder how long that's been there? What does it signify?"

I watched Phoebe bite her trembling lip.

ꛃꛃꛃ

The day we buried Phineas was somber and gloomy, scattered showers peppered our umbrellas. A small contingent; my parents, brothers, and sisters, along with Mother Gage and Phoebe, followed the funeral hearse to Lone Mountain Cemetery. Mud caked to the horse's hooves, flying off in sticky chunks, splashing in the puddles.

The minister's words were blessedly short, perfunctory as we gathered around the open grave, pulling ourselves deeper inside warm coats.

Three grave diggers stood at a distance, leaning against shovels, waiting to begin. As we turned to depart, they approached. They must have been wishing to finish early so they could get warm.

I imagined Phineas laying in his box, cold, and still. That little doll tucked in his breast pocket and the tamping iron resting in the crook of his arm.

I said a prayer, hoping that he was finally at peace. Inside our carriage, I took my wife's hand, bringing her chilled fingers to my lips.

Supervisor Shattuck: San Francisco 1867

Six Years After Phineas's Death

At thirty-seven, San Francisco businessman David D. Shattuck was a newly elected member of the San Francisco Board of Supervisors. Several weeks after taking his seat, the Board unanimously granted him a four-month leave of absence so he could fulfill an unusual request.

David's return to the eastern states began two years earlier when his mother-in-law received a letter from Doctor Harlow. Hannah was delighted to hear from the man she still held in high esteem. She wrote to inform him of her son's passing.

The Doctor responded with condolences, then asked for details. Hannah, in her late sixties, was glad to oblige, reminiscing about the events of her son's life. They corresponded at regular intervals, until the letter came that said, 'the precise condition of the encephalon at the time of his death might have been known had an autopsy been performed.'

For the benefit of science, the doctor asked, would she allow an exhumation of Phineas's head?

David

Mother Gage brought the letter to me, asking if such a thing were possible and how it could be accomplished.

"You're thinking of desecrating the remains of your son?" I was incredulous.

"It is not a desecration, David. Phineas is with God. Doctor Harlow says that the skull would provide a means of scientific discovery. It may be a way to understand why Phineas was sickly after the accident."

"Are you sure?" I asked, in disbelief.

She brought me every letter that Doctor Harlow had sent. The man presented convincing arguments. I could see, now, how she'd come to her conclusions.

I promised Mother Gage that I would make discreet inquiries.

Doctor Henri Coon, the outgoing Mayor of San Francisco, is a colleague and a friend. We've worked together on city projects and share meals at each other's homes. If anyone knew the answer to Mother's questions, it would be him. I brought Harlow's correspondence with me when I arrived at our meeting.

I watched Henri's expressions change as he read one letter after another. When he set the last page upon the stack, he raised his eyes, "Well, David," he said with a cynical smile, "if his mother wishes for this to be done, who are we to argue? I have a few questions for Doctor Harlow that I want you to ask before we consider the matter further."

My stomach dropped. I had hoped that the gruesome task would be out of the question. Now, I knew that I would be responsible for seeing it to its conclusion.

"I would also advise you and your family to not speak of this until after you've been confirmed for your Board seat.

"Yes, of course." I agreed.

ཉཉཉ

I was busy composing a letter to Doctor Harlow when Phoebe came into my office. She'd just finished putting Frank and Alice to bed.

"You look so serious." Phoebe wrapped her arms around my shoulders, leaning in, hugging me. Her eye caught the first lines on the paper, "Doctor Harlow? I know Mother has been corresponding with him; now you are too? Why?"

Setting down my pen, I turned in my chair, "Phoebe, we must talk."

After I explained Harlow's request, her mother's willingness to go along with it, and Doctor Coon's response, Phoebe looked dismayed.

"You should have refused Mother immediately!"

"She asked me to read Doctor Harlow's letters. It was his words, not Mother's, that convinced me."

Phoebe clenched her fists; she paced. I knew that she kept control of her voice for the sake of the children, but I'd never seen her so upset.

"Mother believes Doctor Harlow is a saint. I don't agree. He disregarded my wishes when Phineas was suffering. Doctor Harlow is only looking out for his own interests!"

"Darling," I approached, rubbing her arms. I didn't want her getting upset. Intense emotions could damage the child she was carrying, "if it wasn't for Doctor Harlow, Phineas might have died in forty-eight. He got twelve more years." I pulled my sobbing wife into my arms. "Doctor Harlow says that this will assure his mark in history. If your mother wants her son's memory preserved, we can't say, 'no.'"

Phoebe took the handkerchief that I offered, wiping her tears and her nose. "He tried so hard after the accident to be the man he used to be."

We walked to the divan where we sat close; she snuggled beneath the arm I placed around her shoulders.

Resting her head against me, Phoebe continued, her voice was calmer. "If history remembered him as someone who traveled, adventured, and took a chance at living in a country where he didn't even speak the language, then I would cheer you on. But, David, if we let Harlow have Phineas's head— . You know what Phineas said about his time in Boston and New York."

"I know…" I whispered.

Lone Mountain Cemetery 1867

On a misty morning in November, I found myself in the Lone Mountain Cemetery looking down at my brother-in-law's tombstone. Doctor Coon and Doctor J.B.D. Stillman stood at my side, each with a shovel in hand.

I recalled the grave diggers I'd observed at Phin's burial. The weather had been similar.

Guards stood at the closed entrance gates affording us privacy.

Coats came off as digging commenced. At first, I felt that I was committing an unforgivable sin. But as my back strained and my hands developed blisters, those feelings subsided, until my shovel made contact with something solid.

The other two paused, nodding to one another, then resumed. Once space was clear, the two doctors were about to lift the coffin lid when I interrupted. "Wait! Gentlemen, please bear with my squeamishness. Before you open it, would you prepare me for what I am about to see?"

Doctor Coon looked uncomfortable. He glanced at Doctor Stillman who replied, "Why, David, you need not see anything."

"No," I disagreed firmly. "I promised my wife that I would follow it through to the end."

"She never needs to know," Doctor Coon replied softly.

"I'll know. Please, just tell me."

"Very well," the man sighed as he wiped his hands on his vest, "By now, all of the body fluids will have dissipated. The clothing will be intact. Likely, dry skin will still cover the skeletal remains.

Hair will be present." Coon paused to see how I was taking it. "Shall I describe what we'll do next and the skull removal process?"

Squeezing my eyes shut, I nodded.

"Once the lid is off, the first thing I will do is hand you the iron bar. Next, I will test the skull to see if it separates from the spine. If not, Doctor Stillman has tools for that. I will remove any organic matter that freely separates. Doctor Stillman will take the skull and place it inside the box." Coon paused, waiting for my response.

"Understood. Proceed," I said gravely.

It took all three of us climbing inside the hole to pry the lid up and place it off to the side. I was surprised to see Phineas's body exactly as Doctor Coon described.

Mummified-looking remains wore Phin's clothes. But it no longer looked like the man I remembered. When I hopped out of the hole, Doctor Coon handed up the bar. It was ice-cold to the touch, heavier than I remembered.

Not wishing to watch more of the proceedings, I held it up, running a finger over the words etched on its surface.

This is the bar that was shot through the head of Mr. Phinehas P. Gage at Cavendish, Vermont, Sept. 14, 1848. He fully recovered from the injury & deposited this bar in the Museum of the Medical College of Harvard University. Phinehas P. Gage Lebanon Grafton Cy N-H Jan 6, 1850

I remembered Phin's story about the engraver he hired to do the work, misspelling his name. I could hear Phineas saying, 'When mistakes are made, it's the good man who doesn't get angry, but figures out how to move forward from there.'

I chose to focus on memories rather than listen to the doctors going on about their ghoulish activity.

"Mission accomplished," Doctor Stillman proclaimed loudly, breaking into my thoughts. He and Doctor Coon replaced the coffin lid. "Let's get that hole filled."

When we finished, Doctor Stillman offered to take the skull with him to process it for travel.

I promised myself at that moment, that 'the skull' would remain inside its box until it was delivered to Doctor Harlow. I didn't care to, ever, look at it, or have any member of my family see it.

Without my noticing, a murky fog had rolled in. The city beyond the cemetery walls had been engulfed in a chilly, dull, gray blankness of a November day. Seagulls could be heard high above in the blue sky that must be up there. Our boot steps sounded muffled.

Doctor Stillman cradled the box in front of him like a wise man on his way to deliver a gift to the baby Jesus. Doctor Coon carried shovels and a bag of tools. I kept pace with the others, Phineas's bar grew heavier every minute.

A raven landed on a tombstone nearby. It shrieked, raising its wings like it expected a token in exchange for letting us pass.

When the guards opened the gates, the metal hinges let loose a high-pitched protest. I wondered if the flaming gates of hell would sound that way if this deed took me to that entrance.

Worse yet, would Phoebe ever forgive me for this?

The End

Epilogue

David and Phoebe's Children – Alice, Delia & Frank: San Francisco, March 1890

Twenty-Three Years Later

Spending sunny afternoons picnicking in the cemeteries was common. The decorative monuments radiated the sun's heat, and the Pacific Ocean views were dramatic.

When families came, they congregated in 'their' area. Sisters Delia and Alice perched atop their grandfather Jesse Gage's headstone watching their husbands and older brother playing hide and seek with the children.

Though it was a balmy day, Delia wrapped a blanket tightly around her shoulders. She shivered, "I think I may be coming down with something."

"Maybe…" Alice assessed her younger sister, "you're finally with child."

Waving away the comment, she said, "I received a letter from cousin Ella. She sent a clipping from a New York newspaper. It was an article about a boy who survived a shot to the head. It references Uncle Phineas's injury. At the end of the article, they say that because Uncle joined Barnum's museum, he was known as a freak."

The men and children returned, catching the end of the conversation. "I only have sketchy memories, because I was so young," Frank said. "I was frightened when I first met Uncle Phin. I didn't know what to think about his only having one eye."

"Father shamed me for crying," Frank continued, "he told me that we judge people by what is in their heart, not by how they look."

"Uncle Phineas was fun." Frank smiled. "He gave me my first puppy and played with us kids when the other adults stayed inside. I forgot about his face after a time."

"Mother's abiding resentment toward Father was unfounded, then," ruminated Alice. "Uncle Phineas decided his legacy when he went to work for P.T. Barnum."

"Mother's grudge may have been misguided," Frank said, "but hundreds of orphans and Indian children benefitted from it. Father might not have made those donations if he weren't trying to make it up to her."

Everyone regarded Phineas's headstone. Alice stretched, making a face. "Whenever I look at that, I can't help thinking about what Father did— digging it up."

"I know," Delia frowned. "Sometimes I wish that mother had kept that to herself… I hope that someday another member of the family does something noteworthy, so Uncle Phineas isn't the only one with a claim to fame." She leaned forward, coughing.

ﮞﮞﮞ

The words on Phineas's gravestone, carved in granite, a lasting testament through time, had been chosen by Phoebe. 'Phineas P. Gage 1823 -1860. Adventurer and Pioneer. Beloved son, brother, and uncle.'
Phoebe never saw him as anything other than her brother. In every phase of his life, she loved him.

៙៙៙

Delia Shattuck's gravestone appears on Ocean Beach in San Francisco when heavy storms move sand out to sea. It was last uncovered on June 4, 2012.

To find out more about San Francisco's cemetery removal and its civic uses of the tombstones, continue reading.

Research Sources:

Live links, listed below, are available at http://bit.ly/2rw2KIte.

If you've discovered or unearthed previously unknown information about Phineas Gage – especially as it relates to his time spent in Valparaiso & Santiago, Chile or with Henry Trevitt – contact Malcolm Macmillian.

Malcolm Macmillan is Adjunct Professor at the School of Psychology at Deakin University, Australia. He is the world's Phineas Gage expert.

https://www.uakron.edu/gage/questions.dot?

An Odd Kind of Fame, Stories of Phineas Gage by Malcolm Macmillan.

Harvard Countway Library of Medicine

https://www.countway.harvard.edu/help/who-was-phineas-gage

Warren Anatomical Museum

https://www.countway.harvard.edu/chom/about-collections

Doctor John Harlow's 1868 report to Massachusetts Medical Society – Recovery from the Passage of an Iron Bar Through the Head

https://en.wikisource.org/wiki/Recovery_from_the_passage_of_an_iron_bar_through_the_head

Wikipedia Phineas Gage page

https://en.wikipedia.org/wiki/Phineas_Gage

Wiyot Indian Massacre: 1860 six murderers nearly wiped out the Wiyot Indian tribe

http://www.sfgate.com/entertainment/article/In-1860-six-murderers-nearly-wiped-out-the-Wiyot-2816476.php

San Francisco Cemetery Removal:

In 1902, San Francisco Board of Supervisors disallowed burials within the city limits (Ordinance #8108).

In the 1930's and 1940's, the City of San Francisco evicted the cemeteries, creating a 'pioneer mound' – a mass gravesite – holding forty thousand bodies at Cypress Lawn cemetery in Colma, California.

This is where Phineas and other members of his family eventually came to rest.

Encyclopedia of San Francisco - Removal of San Francisco Cemeteries

http://www.sfhistoryencyclopedia.com/articles/c/cemeteries.html

1950 Location, regulation, and removal of Cemeteries in the City of San Francisco by William A. Proctor

Department of City Planning

City and County of San Francisco

http://www.sfgenealogy.com/sf/history/hcmcpr.htm

A Second Final Rest: The History of San Francisco's Lost Cemeteries film by Trina Lopez

http://trinalopez.com/finalrest.html

KQED Radio Program: Why are all of San Francisco's Dead People Buried in Colma?

https://soundcloud.com/kqed/bay-curious-has-colma-always-been-for-san-franciscos-dead

Transcript:
https://ww2.kqed.org/news/2015/12/16/why-are-so-many-dead-people-in-colma-and-so-few-in-san-francisco/

Bodies found during the construction of San Francisco's Legion of Honor
'Still Rooms' Slide Show by Photographer Richard Barnes –

http://www.richardbarnes.net/still-rooms/mtjfumzj50oowcnkvam1c2ewduv6l5

Cemetery of the Week #145: The Ghost of San Francisco's Laurel Hill

https://cemeterytravel.com/2014/09/03/cemetery-of-the-week-145-the-ghost-of-san-franciscos-laurel-hill/

Delia Presby Shattuck Oliver's Gravestone:

The lettering -- still legible -- reads; Delia Presby, wife of, F.B. Oliver, Died, April 9, 1890, Aged 26 yrs., 10 mos. 27 days. – Rest –

122 Year-old Gravestone Washes Up on Ocean Beach

http://www.missionmission.org/2012/06/04/122-year-old-gravestone-washes-up-on-ocean-beach/

Ocean Beach Headstones – Weird San Francisco History

http://www.sfgate.com/bayarea/article/Tombstones-from-long-ago-surfacing-on-S-F-beach-3618805.php

Find a Grave

http://www.findagrave.com/cgi-bin/fg.cgi?page=gr&GRid=91507663

Tombstone Civic Uses and Appearances:

History of Erosion on Ocean Beach by Bill McLaughlin Surfrider Foundation, San Francisco Chapter

http://public.surfrider.org/files/a_history_of_coastal_erosion_at_ocean_beach_0412.pdf

Removal of San Francisco Cemeteries

By the end of 1948 what was left of the Gage and Shattuck families, along with numerous pioneers who birthed the city of San Francisco, would be disinterred from the Laurel Hill (Lone Mountain renamed) cemetery and moved to a mass gravesite forty miles south in Colma, California.

Tombstones Used in Civic Projects

Thousands of tombstones were recycled and used in a variety of civic projects; the sea wall at Yacht Harbor and breakwaters at the Aquatic Park and Marina Green, construction of the Wave Organ, as fill bedding for the Great Highway, as paving stones in the storm drains at Buena Vista Park, and as erosion control at Ocean Beach.

Stockton Insane Asylum

http://www.sfgate.com/bayarea/article/Historic-asylums-and-sanitariums-of-Northern-8200431.php

Lisa's Online Research Resources:

- **YouTube - Phineas Gage Playlist**

https://www.youtube.com/playlist?list=PL8BKnrxd9IapqfU-NXYLekMNqLjYXMq7T

- **Pinterest - Phineas Gage Books and Articles**

https://www.pinterest.com/lisaredfern17/rail-road-phineas-gage/

- **Pinterest - San Francisco History Research**

https://www.pinterest.com/lisaredfern17/san-francisco-1800s-early-1900s/

San Francisco Map with Gage and Cemetery Related Points of Interest

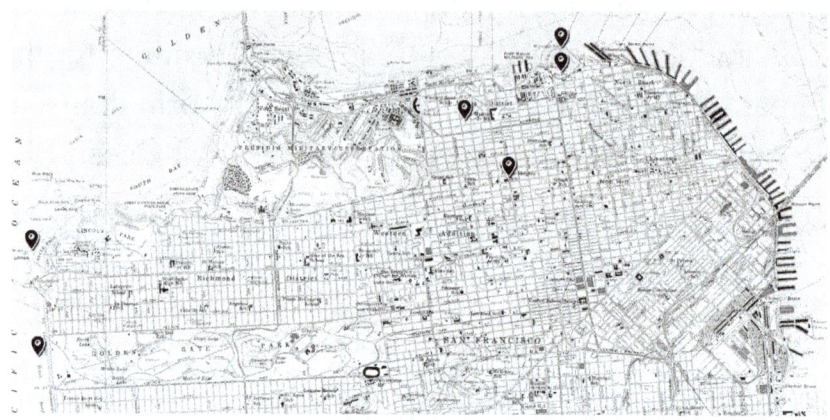

Live links, listed above, (and more historic photos) are available at http://bit.ly/2rw2KIt.

Fictional Story Elements:

Phoebe Gage Shattuck & David Dustin Shattuck photos.

Phoebe's personality and dialog. Her role as family nurse during Phineas's accident recovery. Phoebe's experiences crossing the isthmus and in Panama City.

Phoebe and Hannah's presence at Phineas's sick bed.

 Mr. & Mrs. Adams.

Phineas's friend, Shamus, from his work crew.

It is unknown if Phineas traveled with his sister and parents aboard ship to Chagres.

Witch of the Wave was a ship in service at the time, but it was not the name of the ship that Phoebe and her parents traveled aboard.

Gage family religious practices and family communications.

Photograph of George Anderson.

Friendship between Phineas Gage and George Anderson, the Living Skeleton.

George Anderson's marriage to Hester, the Bearded Lady, and their son.

Phineas's relationship with Caroline.

PTSD-like reaction to blasting sounds in Chagres, Panama.

Phineas's dreams.

The name, James McGill, for the shipping company agent.

Fictional Story Elements continued:

The Gage family friendship with James McGill.

Phoebe's art and her anaconda story.

Phineas's test driving coaches with Mr. McGill and company.

Phineas's story, with memory-like details, of the cowboy and Yaimai.

Graveside scene. [Exhumation of the body, the people involved, removal of the skull and tamping iron are factual.]

Dr.'s Coon and Stillman processing the skull.

Cemetery picnic scene with Alice, Delia, and their brother Frank.

Shattuck donations to orphans and Indian children.

Phoebe's words written on her brother's tombstone.

Lisa

About the Author

Too often, we feel disconnected from history. Black and white photos, museum exhibits, and statistics make us forget that the people who came before us lived full and colorful lives.

"The best and most beautiful things in the world cannot be seen or even touched - they must be felt with the heart." - Helen Keller.

Keller's sentiment is one that Lisa carries through every aspect of her creative work. In her writing, Lisa is exploring history, time travel, relationships and, self-acceptance themes.

She has worked as a professional photographer, a book publicist, a grant writer, and a recycling educator. Lisa earned a Bachelor of Science Degree in Business Administration with a concentration in Marketing from CSU, Sacramento.

She lives in Nevada City, California, a picturesque mining town with plenty of opportunities for outdoor activities. Lisa shares her home with her husband, son, two dogs, two cats, and a beta fish.

www.redfern.biz

Your Feedback is Valuable

If you enjoyed **Gage Facing Forward**,
here's what you can do next.

Leave a brief review on Amazon and / or Goodreads;
a few stars and a couple of words mean a great deal.

Acknowledgments

The first germs for the **Phases of Gage** story were sprouted at the Donner Summit Historical Society while gathering information for another project that includes railroad history, mid-nineteenth century Chinese immigration, and the development of infrastructure in the early days of California.

While many sources were used for research, **An Odd Kind of Fame** by Malcolm Macmillan was the most valuable.

My beta readers can never receive enough gratitude. Their honest opinions and feedback start conversations that broaden my point of view.

Publishing, especially as the writing craft evolves, is a partnership between the author and the editor. Editors help spot holes in the plotline, clarify, dot the i's and cross the t's. Thank you, Hock Tjoa for editing, commenting and thinking about Phineas and his **After the Accident Years**.

Thank you to my family for understanding my need to create, giving me the space to do it, and for bringing me food sometimes.

Lisa Redfern

www.ingramcontent.com/pod-product-compliance
Lightning Source LLC
Chambersburg PA
CBHW060637130626
46555CB00002B/847